D1631688

First published 1996 by Methuen
an imprint of Reed Books Children's Publishing
Michelin House, 81 Fulham Road, London SW3 6RB
and Auckland, Melbourne, Singapore and Toronto.

1 3 5 7 9 10 8 6 4 2

ISBN 1 85591 568 5

Printed in Italy

Winnie-the-Pooh

Invents a New Game

From the Stories by A.A. Milne

With new and adapted illustrations
in the style of E.H. Shepard

METHUEN

One day, as Pooh was walking towards the wooden bridge which crosses the river, he was trying to make up a piece of poetry about fir-cones, because there they were, lying about on each side of him, and he felt singy. So he picked a fir-cone up,

and looked at it, and said to himself, "This is a very good fir-cone, and something ought to rhyme to it." But he couldn't think of anything. And

then this came into his head
suddenly:

Here is a myst'ry
About a little fir-tree.
Owl says it's his tree,
And Kanga says it's her tree.

"Which doesn't make sense," said
Pooh, "because Kanga doesn't live in
a tree."

He had just come to the bridge;
and not looking where he was going,
he tripped over something, and the
fir-cone jerked out of his paw into
the river.

"Bother," said Pooh, as it floated slowly under the bridge, and he went back to get another fir-cone which had a rhyme to it. But then he thought that he would just look at the river instead, because it was a peaceful sort of day, so he lay down and looked at it, and it slipped slowly away beneath him...and suddenly, there was his fir-cone slipping away too.

"That's funny," said Pooh. "I dropped it on the other side," said Pooh, "and it came out on this side! I wonder if it would do it again?" And he went back for some more fir-cones.

It did. It kept on doing it. Then he dropped two in at once, and leant over the bridge to see which of them

would come out first; and one of
them did; but as they were both the
same size, he didn't know if it was
the one which he wanted to win, or
the other one.

And that was the beginning of the game called Poohsticks, which Pooh invented, and which he and his friends used to play on the edge of the Forest. But they played with sticks instead of fir-cones, because

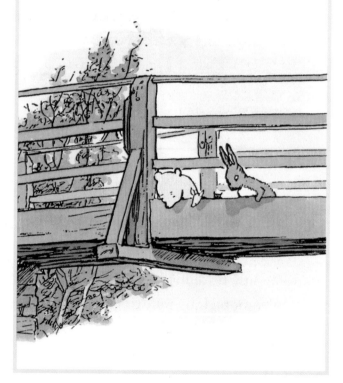

they were easier to mark.

Now one day Pooh and Piglet and Rabbit and Roo were all playing Poohsticks together. They had dropped their sticks in when Rabbit said "Go!" and then they had hurried across to the other side of the bridge, and now they were all leaning over the edge, waiting to see whose stick would come out first.

"I can see mine!" cried Roo. "No, I can't, it's something else. Can you see yours, Piglet? I thought I could see mine, but I couldn't. There it is! No, it isn't. Can you see yours, Pooh?"

"No," said Pooh.

"Mine's a sort of greyish one," said Piglet, not daring to lean too far over in case he fell in.

"Yes, that's what I can see. It's coming over on to my side."

Rabbit leant over further than ever, looking for his, and Roo wriggled up and down, calling out "Come on, stick! Stick, stick, stick!" and Piglet got very excited because his was the only one which had been seen, and that meant that he was winning.

"It's coming!" said Pooh.

"Are you sure it's mine?" squeaked Piglet excitedly.

"Yes, because it's grey. A big grey one. Here it comes! A very – big – grey – Oh, no, it isn't, it's Eeyore."

And out floated Eeyore.

"Eeyore!" cried everybody.

Looking very calm, very dignified, with his legs in the air, came Eeyore from beneath the bridge.

"It's Eeyore!" cried Roo, terribly excited.

"Is that so?" said Eeyore, getting caught up by a little eddy, and turning slowly round three times. "I wondered."

"I didn't know you were playing," said Roo.

"I'm not," said Eeyore.

"Eeyore, what are you doing there?" said Rabbit.

"I'll give you three guesses, Rabbit. Digging holes in the ground? Wrong. Leaping from branch to branch of a young oak-tree? Wrong. Waiting for somebody to help me out of the river? Right. Give Rabbit time, and he'll always get the answer."

"But Eeyore," said Pooh in distress, "what can we – I mean, how shall we – do you think if we –"

"Yes," said Eeyore. "One of those would be just the thing. Thank you, Pooh."

There was a moment's silence while everybody thought.

"I've got a sort of idea," said Pooh at last, "but I don't suppose it's a very good one."

"I don't suppose it is either," said Eeyore.

"Go on, Pooh," said Rabbit. "Let's have it."

"Well, if we all threw stones and things into the river on one side of Eyeore, the stones would make waves, and the waves would wash him to the other side."

"That's a very good idea," said Rabbit, and Pooh looked happy again.

"Very," said Eeyore. "When I want to be washed, Pooh, I'll let you know."

But Pooh had got the biggest stone he could carry, and was leaning over the bridge, holding it in his paws.

"I'm not throwing it, I'm dropping it, Eeyore," he explained. "And then I can't miss – I mean I can't hit you. Could you stop turning round for a moment, because it muddles me rather?"

"No," said Eeyore. "I like turning round."

Pooh dropped his stone. There was a loud splash, and Eeyore disappeared....

And then, just as Pooh was beginning to think that he must have chosen the wrong stone or the wrong river or the wrong day for his Idea, something grey showed for a moment by the river bank...and it got slowly bigger and bigger...and at last it was Eeyore coming out.

With a shout they rushed off the bridge, and pushed and pulled at him; and soon he was standing among them again on dry land.

"Oh, Eeyore, you are wet!" said Piglet, feeling him.

Eeyore shook himself, and asked somebody to explain to Piglet what happened when you had been inside a river for quite a long time.

"How did you fall in, Eeyore?" asked Rabbit, as he dried him with Piglet's handkerchief.

"I was BOUNCED," said Eeyore.

"Oo," said Roo excitedly, "did somebody push you?"

"Somebody BOUNCED me. I was just thinking by the side of the river – thinking, if any of you know what that means – when I received a loud BOUNCE."

"Oh, Eeyore!" said everybody.

"But who did it?" asked Roo.

Eeyore didn't answer.

"I expect it was Tigger," said Piglet nervously.

"But, Eeyore," said Pooh, "was it a Joke, or an Accident? I mean –"

"I didn't stop to ask, Pooh. Even at the very bottom of the river I didn't stop to say to myself, 'Is this a Hearty Joke, or is it the Merest Accident?' I just floated to the surface, and said to myself, 'It's wet.' If you know what I mean."

"And where was Tigger?" asked Rabbit.

Before Eeyore could answer, there was a loud noise behind them, and through the hedge came Tigger himself.

"Hallo, everybody," said Tigger cheerfully.

"Hallo, Tigger," said Roo.

Rabbit became very important suddenly.

"Tigger," he said solemnly, "what happened just now?"

"Just when?" said Tigger a little uncomfortably.

"When you bounced Eeyore into the river."

"I didn't bounce him."

"You bounced me," said Eeyore gruffly.

"I didn't really. I had a cough, and I happened to be behind Eeyore, and I said 'Grr-oppp-ptschschschz.'"

"That's what I call bouncing," said Eeyore. "Taking people by surprise. Very unpleasant habit."

"I didn't bounce, I coughed," said Tigger crossly.

"Bouncy or Coffy, it's all the same at the bottom of the river."

"Well," said Rabbit, "all I can say is – well, here's Christopher Robin, so he can say it."

Christopher Robin came down from the Forest to the bridge, feeling all sunny and careless, and just as if twice nineteen didn't matter a bit, as it didn't on such a happy afternoon.

"It's like this, Christopher Robin," began Rabbit, "Tigger –"

"All I did was I coughed," said Tigger.

"He bounced," said Eeyore.

"Well, I sort of boffed," said Tigger.

"Hush!" said Rabbit, holding up his paw. "What does Christopher Robin think about it all? That's the point."

"Well," said Christopher Robin, not quite sure what it was all about. "I think –"

"Yes?" said everybody.

"I think we all ought to play Poohsticks."

So they did. And Eeyore, who
had never played it before, won
more times than anybody else; and
Roo fell in twice, the first time by
accident and the second time on
purpose, because he suddenly saw
Kanga coming from the Forest, and
he knew he'd have to go to bed

anyhow. So then Rabbit said he'd
go with them; and Tigger and
Eeyore went off together, because
Eeyore wanted to tell Tigger How
to Win at Poohsticks; and
Christopher Robin and Pooh and
Piglet were left on the bridge by
themselves.

For a long time they looked at the river beneath them, saying nothing, and the river said nothing too, for it felt very quiet and peaceful on this summer afternoon.

"Tigger is all right, really," said Piglet lazily.

"Of course he is," said Christopher Robin.

"Everybody is really," said Pooh. "That's what I think," said Pooh. "But I don't suppose I'm right," he said.

"Of course you are." said Christopher Robin.